BLACK BEARD
DRAGON ISLAND

AUTHOR

BY

PEPE GARCIA

Captain Black Beard grinned as the sea breeze rustled through his thick beard. He stood confidently at the helm of The Black Wing, his trusted ship, while his ever-chatty parrot, Backup, perched on his shoulder.

"That was a close one with that scoundrel Red Beard," said Backup, flapping his soaked feathers and shaking his head.

They were homeward bound after a long adventure on Mystery Island.

The skies were calm—until the winds shifted and the ocean darkened. Thunder cracked like cannon fire.
Backup looked up, uneasy. "That's not just weather, Captain."
Then—BOOM!

Lightning struck the sea as The Black Wing fought to stay afloat. Captain Black Beard gritted his teeth and held the wheel steady.
The storm was wild, unrelenting.
A monstrous wave rose like a wall and came crashing down.
The ship spun violently, colliding with something massive beneath the surface.
Wood shattered.
Everything went dark.

When Black Beard awoke, he lay sprawled on a rocky shore.
The remains of The Black Wing lay scattered behind him.
Backup fluttered over, drenched but alive. "You alright, Cap?"
Ahead, a mysterious island stretched out
Thick with jungle, glowing rocks, and an unnatural silence.
"This place feels… ancient," Black Beard muttered.
"And dangerous," Backup added.

Backup dodged fireballs and claw swipings. "Captain—are those, are those DRAGONS?!" Holly moley Dragons exist ?!?!
Another blast singed Black Beard's tricorn hat. "This is no dream, my friend". Snap out of it backup. They fought back, outnumbered but unyielding.

A powerful roar shook the skies.
The darkness above wasn't storm clouds—but wings.
Seven enormous dragons descended, each glowing with raw elemental energy.
The scavenger dragons froze, then fled into the jungle.
Black Beard and Backup stood in awe as the new dragons landed—powerful, majestic, and radiating strength.

The leader, a black-and-silver dragon named Silvex, stepped forward.

"You fought with courage," he rumbled. "But courage alone is not enough."

One by one, the others stepped forward:
- Pyre (Red & White)
- Drakonis (Royal Blue & Light Blue)
- Azmira (teal blue).
- Aurelia (Orange & Yellow)
- Veridion (Forest & Neon Green)
- Chromaris (Chameleon-like, shifting colors)

Together, they were known as The Seven Eternal Flames of Alphael.

"I seek no trouble," said Black Beard. "Just safe passage home."

Silvex narrowed his eyes. "You've touched the heart of dragon island. It will now test you."

To prove themselves, Black Beard and Backup followed the dragons into the jungle.

The deeper they went, the stranger the terrain. The Trees were breathing. The air became warm & smelled of volcanic ash. The island itself was alive.

From a lava river ahead, a giant obsidian rock monster emerged—taller than the trees, magma dripping from its shoulders.
Its red eyes locked onto them as it raised a molten fist.
Black Beard dodged, slashing where he could.
"Cap! Its back!" Backup called.
Using a thick vine and a bit of clever maneuvering, they distracted it long enough for Black Beard to strike the glowing core on its spine.
The creature collapsed with a steaming crash.

The Seven dragons looked on, impressed.
"You've passed the first trial," said Azmira. "But now comes the second—in fire."
They soared toward a distant volcano, its peak glowing a dangerous red.
Black Beard and Backup followed into Infernal Hollow, where the ground trembled and the air shimmered with heat.

Inside, they were tasked with retrieving a Crystal Egg, a powerful relic hidden within the blazing heart of the lava chambers and guarded by an ancient fire wraith born from the island's core.

"Only those with unshakable will and sharp minds can claim it," warned Aurelia.

The guardian emerged—an ethereal inferno shaped like a dragon, its body composed of roaring flame and swirling embers, its eyes two burning coals of hatred and hunger.

Black Beard spotted a reflective shard from the shipwreck lodged in the cavern wall. Thinking quickly, he drew his sword and angled the shard, casting a blinding flare of redirected light into the fire wraith's face. The creature recoiled, its form flickering wildly.

Seizing the moment, Black Beard dove through a wall of flame, snatched the glowing Crystal Egg from its pedestal, and rolled to safety as the chamber quaked with the wraith's roar of frustration.

As the egg pulsed with power, a cold shadow swept across the volcano.
Smoke formed into the shape of a colossal dragon cloaked in mist.
"It's him..." whispered Chromaris.
Its Obscurion.
The villainous dragon hovered above them, his eyes burning with twisted hunger.
"Give me the Crystal Egg," he growled.

"Never," Black Beard replied.

Obscurion laughed. "Dragon Island is mine. I will destroy the egg—and with it, this prison. The world will kneel."

He summoned seven corrupted dragons—dark, monstrous reflections of the Seven Flames.

The sky turned to chaos.

Each of the Seven Flames faced their opposite:
- Pyre's twin breathed smoke and decay.
- Drakonis clashed with a cold-hearted version of himself.
- Azmira met a shadowed force that drained color from the sky.

And so, dragon against dragon, power against power.

Just as the eternal flames of Alphael appeared to be loosing..
A blinding white flash split the clouds.
Descending with wings of crystal light came Alphael—the legendary white dragon.
"You've lost your soul, obscurion," he said.
"Then try to stop me," Obscurion snarled.
Their clash of light and shadow shook the heavens.

Thunder cracked in the absence of clouds, and the heavens themselves seemed to rip open. Black Beard and Backup crouched on a high ledge, the Crystal Egg glowing faintly in Backup's talons like a beating heart.

Blurs of motion streaked through the storm-wracked sky—claws clashing, tails whipping, roars thundering louder than cannon fire. The dragons hurled themselves at one another with primal fury, leaving trails of scorched sky and shattered light in their wake.

Each collision sent shockwaves across the island, rattling the ledge beneath them. The clash of light and shadow above wasn't just a battle—it was a reckoning.

With a mighty cry, Alphael released a thunderclap from his wings.
The dark dragons were flung backward.
Obscurion hissed and vanished into the clouds.
The Seven Eternal Flames, battered but victorious, returned to the volcano's edge.
Chromaris took the Crystal Egg and flew to the peak of The Eternal Volcano—the island's heart—and dropped it into the white lava.
A golden pulse erupted. The island shimmered—and vanished from view.
Dragon Island was cloaked once more.

The Seven Flames gathered around Black Beard and Backup. "For your bravery and loyalty," said Alphael, "we grant you the gifts of our kind."

He touched Black Beard's shoulder with his glowing claw.

Black Beard felt warmth surge through him—wounds healing, strength returning.

Alphael summoned a blade of obsidian, its edge sharper than diamond, pulsing with fire.

"This cutlass is forged from the island's core. It obeys your will and answers your command with lava."

Alphael then turned to Backup.
"For you, a gift of life."
He placed a golden dragon egg in Backup's wings.
Inside it lay a surprise—one that would awaken only in a moment of great need.
"Use it wisely."
The dragons smiled, proud and solemn.
Drakonis approached Black Beard. "We wish you well on your next journey.

With the help of the dragons, a new ship was forged from enchanted wood, molten ore, and dragon scales.
Stronger, faster, and seemingly indestructible, Ah .. I will call her The Dragon Wing. In honor of our new friends.
Black Beard stood at the helm once more, healed and ready.
The Seven Eternal Flames of Alphael soared overhead one final time.
Alphael's voice echoed:
"Guard your gifts. And beware the Bermuda Triangle."
The wind filled the sails as The Dragon Wing pushed off from the hidden shore.
The ocean stretched ahead. A new mystery awaited.
"Fortune favors the bold," Black Beard said.
Backup nodded. "Let's do this".

ABOUT THE BOOK

Black Beard: Dragon Island follows the daring pirate Captain Black Beard and his loyal parrot, Backup, as they are stranded on a mysterious island filled with dragons, elemental powers, and dark secrets. When the villainous dragon Obscurion threatens the world, Black Beard must face powerful trials and form an unlikely alliance with the Seven Eternal Flames, the island's ancient protectors.

Filled with adventure, magical creatures, and fierce battles, this thrilling tale will take readers on an unforgettable journey of courage, friendship, and survival.

THE END

Dedication

To the dreamers and adventurers who dare to chase the unknown, and to the storytellers who bring magic to life.

May you always find courage, even in the darkest of storms.

Pepe Garcia would like to also dedicate this book to his nieces and nephews: Sophia, Lupita, Ariana, Adrian, & Fernando.

Copyright © 2025

Pepe Garcia

ISBN:

979-8-89795-577-0

979-8-89795-578-7

979-8-89795-579-4

All Rights Reserved. Any unauthorized reprint or use of this material is strictly prohibited. No part of this book may be reproduced or transmitted in any form or by any means, electronic or mechanical, including photocopying, recording, or by any information storage and retrieval system without express written permission from the author.

All reasonable attempts have been made to verify the accuracy of the information provided in this publication. Nevertheless, the author assumes no responsibility for any errors and/or omissions.

Printed in Dunstable, United Kingdom